I0768859

Sanguine

RYEN SANTANA

Title: Sanguine

Author: Ryen Santana

Paperback ISBN: 979-8-9906716-7-6

Disclaimer: This work does not aim to glorify or romanticize the historical figure of Jack the Ripper or the crimes attributed to him. Rather, it serves as an exploration of psychological horror and dark fantasy, incorporating both real and imagined elements to create a complex narrative about madness, guilt, and the supernatural.

For permissions and inquiries, contact: Ryen Santana

Edited by: Stacey's Bookcorner Editing Services

Formatted by: InkSpark Digital

Artwork by: Joanna Sasara, Asnnn Art.

Cover by: GetCovers

Content Warnings

This novel contains explicit depictions of graphic violence, including brutal murders, mutilation, and bloodshed, as well as themes of mental illness, paranoia, and hallucinations. Gender-based violence is a central focus, with the historical crimes against women during the Jack the Ripper era playing a key role. The story also explores themes of death, grief, and the haunting presence of the dead, while incorporating supernatural elements such as ghostly apparitions and demonic style forces. Reader discretion is advised.

If you'd like a more comprehensive list of trigger warnings before you read, please reach out to me on social media or via my website.

From the deepest, most depraved, macabre and disgusting places in my mind is where this came from. So, this isn't a romance by any means. If that is what you're expecting like my usual novels, I'm sorry this isn't it. Feel free to read A Veil of Twilight though hahaha.

To the women whose lives were unjustly taken by darkness, both known and unknown—this is for you. May history remember your names, not the one who stole them.

In an era lacking forensic science and fingerprinting, the sole method of establishing someone's culpability in a homicide was to catch them in the act or elicit a confession from the accused. Regrettably, the Whitechapel Murders took place during this time period.

Chapter One
The Truth

It started with Mary Ann Nichols, though they'll tell you differently. They'll say I did it, that I was the one with the knife. But when I found her, throat open to the bone, the blood still warm, I knew what had killed her wasn't human. I could smell it—the rot, the cold. It hung in the air like death itself had walked those streets, and maybe it had.

I stood above her, just staring. Her eyes were glassy, empty, and her skin was pale and waxy under the flickering gaslight. I could feel it then, the same presence that had been haunting me for months. Something watched from the shadows, unseen, just beyond my reach. The cold crept into my bones, and I knew. I knew this wasn't my crime. This was something else—something older, darker.

The city didn't know it yet, but it was under siege.

The press called me a monster. The Butcher of Whitechapel, they screamed. Jack the Ripper. They plastered my name across every paper, every street corner, turning me into their devil. I might have laughed at the absurdity of it, if the truth weren't so much worse.

I wasn't hunting women. I was hunting for something that shouldn't exist, something that prowled under the cover of night, wearing the fog like a cloak.

I had felt it then, felt it watching as Annie Chapman's body was dragged from Hanbury Street, her abdomen laid open, her insides arranged like some grotesque offering. But the knife hadn't been in my hand. I'd arrived too late, the real killer vanishing into the mist like it was never there at all.

I could hear my pulse in my ears now, the thrum of blood that always came when I was close. That cold prickle on my skin told me it was watching again, somewhere nearby, waiting. I swallowed hard, trying to shake the feeling, but it clung to me like the fog, twisting around my chest, tightening.

And then I felt it... it was close. The weight in the air shifted, and my heart skipped a beat.

The street was empty, but I wasn't alone. I could feel the thing lurking in the fog, just out of sight, waiting.

My fingers tightened around the knife beneath my coat, the steel a poor defense against something that didn't bleed. My pulse quickened, and my breath fogged the air. I hadn't yet seen it for what it truly was, but I had glimpsed it enough to know that this was no man. It was a shadow, a wraith, something pulled from the very darkness of this cursed city. And it had a taste for blood.

The fog swirled unnaturally, a slow, deliberate movement. My throat tightened. I wasn't imagining it. This wasn't the city's usual haze. It was watching me.

Suddenly, I felt something behind me, a faint brush against the back of my neck. I spun, knife drawn, eyes wide, but there was nothing there. Just empty space. The fog closed in, choking, suffocating, and for a moment, I thought it was going to swallow me whole. My breath came fast now, sharp and ragged, and the sound of it filled my ears.

I squinted into the gloom, straining to see, but the mist twisted and writhed like it had a mind of its own, hiding whatever stalked me.

I blinked, and there it was– a shadow within the shadow– moving. Slow. Deliberate.

A figure.

At first, I thought it might be another man, another poor soul wandering these cursed streets. But as it drew closer, I saw the truth.

No man moved like that, so fluid, so silent. It was almost as if it wasn't walking, but floating. Its form was indistinct, a blur of black and gray, merging with the fog.

My breath hitched as it came into focus—an eyeless face, pale as death, with skin stretched too thin over bones that jutted sharply beneath. Its mouth... Christ, its mouth was a gash, black and gaping, like a void where teeth should have been. I couldn't move. I couldn't breathe. My body was frozen in place, locked in terror.

I wanted to tell myself this wasn't real, that my mind was playing tricks on me. But I knew better. This was real

—it was real—and it was hunting me. Just as it had hunted those women.

Then it lunged.

I barely had time to react, diving to the side as its hand shot past me, cold as ice, grazing my arm. The touch burned, a searing, unnatural cold that bit through my coat, through my skin. My knees hit the cobblestones, pain shooting up through my legs, but I didn't care. I scrambled back to my feet, heart hammering, the knife still clenched in my hand.

The thing was gone. The fog had swallowed it again, leaving nothing but silence behind.

My chest heaved, every breath like fire in my lungs, but I knew better than to let my guard down. I wiped the sweat from my brow, though the night was freezing. My coat felt heavier, like the weight of that touch still lingered.

My arm stung where it had grazed me, the skin beneath my coat icy to the touch. It had marked me, claimed me in some way. I could feel the cold deep in my bones now, a chill that no fire could chase away.

I stood there for what felt like an eternity, staring into the fog, waiting for it to return. It didn't. But I knew, I knew, it was still there, watching from the shadows, waiting for the moment I let my guard down. I had to move. I had to find out what this thing was. The city thought I was the one responsible for the murders, that I was some madman butchering women in the streets.

But this wasn't madness. This was real. This was something far worse than any man could dream up.

The police wouldn't believe me. They were too busy chasing shadows of their own, following the trail of blood I had tried so desperately to avoid. They wouldn't understand. They couldn't understand. But I knew what walked these streets. I had seen it. Felt it.

And now it was hunting me.

I adjusted my coat, pulling the collar up against the biting cold. The streets stretched out before me, empty and silent, the fog hiding whatever lurked within. Somewhere out there, the thing was waiting. It had already claimed its victims, and I was next. But I would not let it win.

I wasn't just running from the law anymore. I was running from something far worse, something I didn't fully understand but was determined to stop.

The city believed I was the monster. Let them think that. They didn't know the truth. They didn't know what truly haunted the fog.

I did.

And it was time to hunt it down.

Chapter Two
Into The Underworld

The night clung to the air thick with rot and damp. Each breath felt like inhaling the city's decay, a reminder of the filth that covered every brick, every alleyway, every soul. I could feel it seeping into me, as if the fog itself carried a disease, a sickness that lived within the bones of the city. Whitechapel, especially, was a place where darkness walked freely, without need for shadow or cover. It *thrived* here, fed by the misery of the people, by the blood that had spilled in these alleys for centuries.

The city's underbelly was slick with it.

I moved through the winding streets, the stench of unwashed bodies, waste, and soot filling my nostrils. The gaslights flickered overhead, struggling to pierce the night, their dim light casting distorted, wavering shadows on the damp cobblestones.

I pulled my coat tighter, though it wasn't the cold that chilled me. No, it was something far deeper—a sense that the world was slipping away from me, that everything I thought I knew, everything I could *see*, was being distorted by the darkness I hunted. Or perhaps it was hunting me.

I was going deeper now. Into the heart of something darker than the fog, darker than the murders that had turned me into a monster in the eyes of the world. Into the underworld of London, where things far worse than men made their homes. I had heard whispers of it before, in the opium dens and back alleys, from men whose eyes had seen things that no sane mind could accept. There were forces in this city, they said, ancient forces that had been here long before men built their crumbling streets. Forces that *wanted* blood. And now, I knew those whispers were true.

The woman I sought was said to live in a part of the city no one visited unless they had no other choice. A decaying building, more ruin than home, filled with relics of a time long past. She was a seer, or so they said, though most would call her a witch. I didn't care what she was— witch, seer, demon—I needed answers.

Answers that no one else could give me.

As I turned the corner onto the narrow, filthy lane that led to her dwelling, I could feel eyes watching from the shadows. Rats scurried through the gutters, their claws clicking against the stones, but it wasn't the rats that made my skin crawl. No, it was something else. Something unseen just out of sight, like a predator waiting for its moment to strike.

Her door was unmarked, just a sagging piece of wood

barely hanging on its hinges. I hesitated for a moment, my hand hovering above the worn handle. It felt like crossing a threshold, like stepping into a place where the rules of the world no longer applied. But I had no choice. I had come too far.

Inside the room was dimly lit by candles, their flickering flames casting eerie shadows on the walls, which were lined with shelves crammed with relics and artifacts. Skulls, bones, jars filled with strange substances I couldn't begin to name. The floor was covered in ancient, threadbare rugs, their patterns long since faded.

And in the center of the room, sitting at a low table cluttered with runes and strange symbols, was the woman. She was old—so old it seemed impossible that she still lived. Her skin hung loose from her bones, wrinkled and thin, like parchment. Her eyes, milky and clouded, fixed on me as I stepped inside, though I doubted she could truly see me.

"You've come to find the truth," she said, her voice a rasping whisper that seemed to come from everywhere and nowhere at once.

I nodded, though I wasn't sure how she could know that. "I *need* answers."

She gestured to the chair opposite her, and I sat. My hands clenched into fists under the table, trying to steady the tremor in my fingers. The room felt too small, the air too thick, as though the very walls were pressing in on me, suffocating me.

She reached out, her gnarled fingers brushing against the edge of a bone-white skull on the table. "There are dark forces at work in this city. Forces older than you can imagine."

"I know that," I replied, my voice harsher than I intended. "I've seen them. Felt them."

She smiled then, a slow, creaking movement that sent a shiver down my spine. "You've only seen the shadows. What you hunt is far more dangerous than you know."

"Tell me what it is," I demanded. "Tell me how to stop it."

Her eyes—those blind, cloudy eyes—seemed to pierce straight through me. "There are those who walk between life and death. They've summoned something, opened a door that should never have been opened. These murders —" her voice dropped lower, "—they are not random. They are part of a ritual. A ritual to open a gateway."

A cold chill washed over me, colder than anything the fog outside could conjure. A gateway. I had suspected something dark was at play, but this... this was far worse than I had imagined.

"What kind of gateway?" I asked, though the words barely formed on my lips.

"A gateway to the underworld," she said. "To a place where the dead walk among the living. Where the veil between this world and the next is so thin, it can be torn apart with blood."

Blood. Of course. I had seen enough of it to know that death clung to these streets like a parasite, feeding on the misery, on the violence that the city bred. But this... this was something far worse than I could have imagined.

I swallowed hard, trying to keep the rising panic from

showing on my face. "And who is doing this? Who is behind the murders?"

She shook her head, her eyes never leaving mine. "You already know the answer to that."

I stared at her, my mind racing. I felt my heart pounding against my ribs, each beat echoing in my ears. Did I know? The faces of the victims flashed through my mind, their dead eyes accusing. I saw my own hands stained with ink—or was it blood?

"No," I whispered, more to myself than to her.

The old woman leaned forward, her breath reeking of decay. "The line between hunter and hunted is thinner than you think, Jack. You've been walking it for so long, you can no longer see which side you're on."

I stumbled to my feet, knocking over the chair behind me. The room seemed to spin, the flickering shadows on the walls taking on grotesque shapes. "You're lying," I hissed.

But even as I spoke, doubt gnawed at the edges of my mind. How many nights had I woken, covered in sweat, with no memory of where I'd been? How often had I found myself in places I couldn't remember going to, my clothes stained with something dark that I told myself was just mud?

The old woman's laughter filled the room, a dry, rattling sound like bones clicking together. "Oh, but it is you, Jack. And it isn't. You're just a puppet, dancing on strings you can't even see."

I backed away, my hand fumbling for the door. "No,"

I said again, but my voice lacked conviction. "I'm trying to stop this. I'm trying to save people."

"Are you?" she asked, her milky eyes seeming to follow me. "Or are you just playing your part in a game far older than you can comprehend?"

I fled then, bursting out of the door and into the fog-shrouded street. I ran, my feet pounding against the cobblestones, my lungs burning as I gulped in the putrid air. But no matter how far or fast I ran, I couldn't escape the growing certainty that the old woman's words had planted in my mind.

The fog swirled around me, and for a moment, I swore I could see faces in it—the faces of the dead, their mouths open in silent screams.

I stumbled to a halt, bracing myself against a grimy wall. My hand came away wet, and when I looked down, I saw it was covered in something dark and sticky. Blood? Or just my imagination?

A name surfaced in my mind then, rising from the depths of memory like a corpse floating to the surface of the Thames. A man I'd seen in the shadows, always just out of reach. The one that was behind it all.

Arthur.

I know it was him.

I saw him, that's it.

The name echoed in my mind, a whisper that grew louder with each passing second. Arthur. The Phantom. I had seen him, hadn't I? In the shadows, always lurking just beyond my grasp. His piercing blue eyes haunting my dreams, his smooth voice dripping with malice.

I pushed myself off the wall, stumbling forward through the fog. The streets seemed to shift and change around me, familiar corners suddenly alien and threatening. I needed proof.

My footsteps quickened as I made my way through the twisting alleys, my mind racing. There had to be something I'd overlooked, some clue that would lead me to Arthur and prove my own innocence.

I stumbled through the foggy streets, my mind reeling. *Elizabeth Stride.* The name echoed in my head, a grim portent of what was to come. I had to find her before he did. Before Arthur could claim another victim.

The cobblestones were slick beneath my feet as I made my way to Berner Street. I knew her habits, her routines. She would be there, plying her trade in the shadows. My breath came in ragged gasps, my lungs burning with each inhalation of the putrid air.

As I rounded the corner, I saw her. *Elizabeth.* She was leaning against a wall, her face hidden in shadow. My heart pounded in my chest as I approached. I had to warn her, and save her from the fate that awaited.

"Elizabeth," I called out, my voice hoarse. She turned, her eyes widening with recognition or fear—I couldn't tell which.

"Stay back," she hissed, backing away. "I know who you are."

I froze, confusion washing over me. "No, you don't understand. I'm here to help you. There's danger—"

But my words were cut short as a figure emerged

from the fog behind her. Tall, lean, with piercing blue eyes that seemed to glow in the darkness. Arthur.

"Well, well," he said, his voice smooth as silk. "What have we here?"

Elizabeth whirled around, a scream building in her throat. But before she could utter a sound, Arthur's hand shot out, gripping her neck. I lunged forward, desperate to stop him, but my limbs felt leaden, unresponsive.

"You're too late, Jack," Arthur sneered. "As always."

I watched in horror as he pulled Elizabeth into the shadows. Her terrified eyes locked with mine for a brief moment before she vanished into the darkness. I tried to follow, but my legs gave out beneath me. I collapsed to the ground, the world spinning around me.

When I came to, I found myself kneeling in a pool of blood. Elizabeth's lifeless body lay before me, her throat savagely cut. And in my hand, I clutched a bloody knife.

I found her first, I *always* found them first. *He* led me to them.

"No," I whispered, dropping the weapon as if it had burned me. "This isn't possible."

But as I stared at my blood-stained hands, doubt gnawed at the edges of my mind. Where is Arthur?

The sound of approaching footsteps jolted me back to reality. I scrambled to my feet, casting one last anguished look at Elizabeth's body before fleeing into the night. The fog swallowed me whole, leaving behind only questions and the sickening certainty that this nightmare was far from over.

I stumbled through the fog-shrouded streets, my

mind reeling from what I had just witnessed—or thought I had witnessed. The image of Elizabeth's lifeless body, her throat savagely cut, burned in my vision. And the feel of the knife in my hand... I shuddered, trying to banish the memory.

The distant sound of police whistles pierced the night air, growing closer with each passing moment. I quickened my pace, my heart pounding in my chest. I couldn't be caught, not now. Not when I was so close to unraveling this dark mystery.

I ducked into a narrow alley, pressing myself against the slimy brick wall as a group of constables ran past, their boots splashing through the puddles. As their footsteps faded, I allowed myself to breathe again.

"You're slipping, Jack," a smooth voice whispered from the shadows.

I whirled around, my eyes straining to pierce the darkness. There, at the far end of the alley, stood a tall, lean figure. Even in the dim light, I could see the glint of his piercing blue eyes.

"Arthur," I hissed, my hands clenching into fists.

He stepped forward, his impeccable suit a stark contrast to the filth surrounding us.

"Did you find my gift, Jack?"

"Gift?" I spat, bile rising in my throat. "You call that butchery a gift?"

Arthur's lips curled into a cruel smile. "Oh, but it is. Each death brings us closer to our goal. Can't you feel it, Jack? The veil is thinning, the power growing."

I lunged at him, blind rage overtaking me. But my

hands grasped only empty air as Arthur seemed to melt into the shadows.

His laughter echoed off the damp walls. "Still so impulsive. So... human. You disappoint me, Jack. I had such high hopes for you."

"I'm nothing like you," I snarled, spinning around, trying to locate the source of his voice.

"Aren't you?" Arthur's words seemed to come from everywhere at once. "We're more alike than you care to admit. Two sides of the same coin, you and I. Both walking the line between worlds."

"No," I whispered, shaking my head violently. "You're lying. You're the killer, not me. I saw you... I saw you kill Elizabeth."

"Did you?" Arthur's voice was closer now, a whisper in my ear. "Or did you see what you wanted to see?"

I whirled around, but the alley was empty. Only the fog and the distant sound of police whistles remained.

Doubt gnawed at me, eating away at my certainty like acid. Had I truly seen Arthur kill Elizabeth? Or had I... No. I couldn't let myself think that way. I had to focus, had to find proof.

With trembling hands, I reached into my coat pocket, pulling out a crumpled piece of paper. On it, I had scrawled the address of a warehouse near the docks. A place where, according to my investigations, Arthur conducted his dark rituals.

I set off through the winding streets, my mind racing. If I could find evidence there, proof of Arthur's involvement, I could end this nightmare once and for all.

But as I walked, Arthur's words echoed in my head. "Two sides of the same coin." What did he mean? And why did those words fill me with such dread?

The warehouse loomed before me, a hulking shadow against the night sky. As I approached, I could feel a change in the air, a heaviness that seemed to press down on me. The veil between worlds was thin here, I could sense it.

With shaking hands, I pushed open the rusted door. The hinges creaked, the sound echoing in the cavernous space. Inside, the air was thick with the scent of incense and something darker, more coppery.

My eyes adjusted to the gloom, and I saw them. Symbols painted on the floor in what looked disturbingly like blood. Candles arranged in intricate patterns. And in the center, a circle of salt surrounding a strange, pulsing object.

I approached cautiously, my heart pounding in my chest. The object seemed to throb with an unholy light, pulsing in time with some unseen heartbeat. As I drew closer, I could make out its form—a grotesque amalgamation of bone and flesh, twisted into an unnatural shape.

My stomach churned as recognition dawned. I had seen something like this before, in the darkest corners of my mind, in fever dreams that left me gasping and drenched in sweat. But to see it here, in the physical world...

"Beautiful, isn't it?" Arthur's voice cut through the silence, causing me to spin around. He stood in the door way, his tall frame silhouetted against the fog outside.

"What is that... thing?" I demanded, my voice shaking despite my efforts to steady it.

Arthur stepped into the warehouse, his footsteps echoing in the cavernous space. "That, my dear Jack, is the key to opening the gateway. A beacon to guide the dead back to our world."

I backed away, my eyes darting between Arthur and the pulsing abomination. "You're mad. This is madness."

"Is it?" Arthur's lips curled into a cruel smile. "Or is it the ultimate sanity? To tear down the veil between life and death, to harness powers beyond mortal comprehension?" He moved closer, his piercing blue eyes locked on mine. "You've felt it, haven't you? The pull of the other side. The whispers in the dark. You're drawn to it, just as I am."

I shook my head violently, trying to deny his words. But deep down, I knew there was truth in them. I had always been fascinated by the macabre, by the thin line between life and death. It was what drove me to investigate these murders, to seek out the darkness lurking in London's shadows.

"I'm nothing like you," I spat, but the words sounded hollow even to my own ears.

Arthur laughed, a chilling sound that seemed to reverberate through my very bones. "Oh, but you are. We're two halves of a whole, Jack. The scientist and the artist. The mind and the hand. Together, we will usher in a new age of darkness."

As he spoke, the pulsing object began to glow brighter, its unholy light casting twisted shadows across the warehouse floor. The air grew thick, charged with an energy that made my skin crawl.

"It's beginning," Arthur whispered, his eyes gleaming with a fanatical light. "The gateway is opening."

I watched in horror as the circle of salt began to shift, forming intricate patterns that hurt my eyes to look at directly. The pulsing object rose into the air, suspended by some unseen force.

"Stop this," I pleaded, though I knew my words were futile. "You don't know what you're doing."

Arthur turned to me, "I know *exactly* what I'm doing."

I lunged at Arthur, desperate to stop whatever madness he had set in motion. But as my fingers grasped at his coat, he seemed to shimmer and fade, like smoke dissipating in the wind. His laughter echoed through the warehouse as I stumbled, off-balance.

"Too late, Jack," his voice taunted from everywhere and nowhere. "The ritual has begun."

The pulsing object at the center of the salt circle began to spin, faster and faster until it was a blur of sickening light. The air crackled with energy, making my hair stand on end. I could feel something pressing against the fabric of reality, straining to break through.

Suddenly, the warehouse was plunged into an unnatural darkness. The only light came from the spinning object, casting grotesque, writhing shadows on the walls. And in those shadows, I saw... things. Shapes that should not exist. Faces contorted in eternal agony.

"Do you see them, Jack?" Arthur's voice whispered in

my ear, though I could not see him. "The souls of the damned, clawing their way back to our world. And soon, they will walk among us once more."

A scream built in my throat as I watched ethereal hands reach out from the spinning vortex, grasping at the air. The stench of decay filled my nostrils, and I could taste ash on my tongue.

The spinning object suddenly exploded in a burst of blinding light. I was thrown backward, my head cracking against the warehouse floor. As my vision swam, I saw... impossibility.

Shadowy figures emerged from the light, their forms flickering and insubstantial. They moved with an unnatural grace, drifting across the floor without leaving footprints in the dust. Their faces were a blur of features, constantly shifting and changing.

And at their center stood Arthur, his arms spread wide in welcome. "Come," he intoned, his voice resonating with power. "Cross over and claim this world as your own."

I tried to move, to stop him, but my limbs felt leaden. The world spun around me as darkness crept in at the edges of my vision. The last thing I saw before unconsciousness claimed me was Arthur turning to face me, his eyes glowing with an otherworldly light.

"Welcome to the new world, Jack," he said, his smile full of cruel promise. "Our world."

Then everything went black.

& SON

Chapter Three
Witching Hour

The putrid stench of blood assaulted my nostrils, pulling me back into consciousness. My head throbbed with each heartbeat, causing waves of agony to crash through my body. As my vision slowly cleared, I realized with horror where I was.

The cobblestones beneath me were slick and slippery, coated in a thick layer of blood. And lying in front of me, like a macabre centerpiece, was the lifeless body of Catherine Eddowes. Her eyes, wide and unseeing, seemed to accuse me as her mutilated form lay sprawled on the ground.

I scrambled away from her, trying to escape this nightmare. But no matter how hard I tried to distance myself from the gruesome scene, the evidence pointed straight at me. My clothes drenched in crimson, and clutched in my hand was a bloody knife—the same one I had seen after Elizabeth Stride's murder.

My mind spun with panic and confusion. How could

this be happening again? How did Arthur place me at the scene of his monstrous crimes every time?

My thoughts were interrupted by approaching foot-steps. Desperate to flee, I turned towards the exit but was met by a figure emerging from the shadows—Arthur.

His smooth voice cut through the tense silence. "My dear Jack," he said, amusement lacing his words. "You've truly outdone yourself this time."

Rage boiled inside of me as I lunged towards him, ready to unleash all of my fury on the man responsible for these horrors. But my hands passed through him as if he were made of mist. His laughter echoed in my ears as he taunted me with his lies and manipulations. "I will always win," he sneered.

The world seemed to tilt beneath my feet. I stumbled, my back hitting the cold brick wall behind me. "No," I whispered, but the word held no conviction.

In the distance, I heard the shrill sound of police whistles. Arthur's form began to fade, merging with the shadows.

"Run, Jack," he said, his voice growing fainter.

As he vanished, I was left alone with the body of Catherine Eddowes and the damning evidence of my guilt. The whistles grew louder, closer.

With one last anguished look at the scene of carnage, I turned and fled into the fog-shrouded streets of London.

The fog swallowed me as I fled, my feet pounding against the slick cobblestones. Each ragged breath burned in my lungs, tasting of ash and decay. The whis-tles of the police faded behind me, but their echoes seemed to chase me through the twisting alleys of Whitechapel.

My mind reeled, unable to reconcile the horrors I had witnessed with my own actions. The image of Catherine Eddowes' mutilated body was seared into my vision, accusing me with every blink. But how could I have done such a thing? I was trying to stop the killings, not perpetrate them.

Yet the evidence was damning. The blood on my clothes, the knife in my hand—all pointed to my guilt. And Arthur... Arthur who appeared and vanished like smoke, always one step ahead, always taunting me.

Framing me.

I stumbled to a halt in a narrow alley, my back pressed against the damp bricks as I fought to catch my breath. The shadows seemed to writhe around me, taking on grotesque shapes that matched the horrors in my mind.

"What is happening to London?" I whispered to the darkness.

As if in answer, a chill wind gusted through the alley, carrying with it the whispers of the dead. I could almost see them—spectral forms reaching out with grasping fingers, their faces contorted in eternal agony. The veil between worlds was thinning, just as Arthur had said. And somehow, I was playing a part in its unraveling.

A sob caught in my throat as the full weight of my situation crashed down upon me. I was lost, adrift in a sea of blood and madness. Every step I took to uncover the truth only seemed to drag me deeper into the abyss.

The distant tolling of church bells cut through my despair. Midnight. The witching hour. A time when the barrier between worlds grew even weaker.

I pushed myself away from the wall, my legs unsteady beneath me. I couldn't give up now. There had to be a way to stop Arthur, to close the gateway he was opening. Even if it meant confronting the darkest parts of myself.

With grim determination, I set off through the fog-shrouded streets.

The city seemed to shift and change around me, familiar streets suddenly alien and threatening. Reality itself felt fragile, as if it might shatter at any moment. And through it all, I could hear Arthur's mocking laughter, calling me ever deeper into the heart of darkness.

I found myself in a part of the city I didn't recognize, though something about it tugged at the edges of my memory. The buildings loomed impossibly tall, their windows dark and accusing. Shadows slithered across the cobblestones, always just out of sight when I turned to look.

A figure appeared at the end of the street, a woman in a tattered dress, her back to me. My breath caught in my throat as I recognized her silhouette.

"Mary?" I called out, my voice hoarse.

She turned, and I recoiled in horror. Her face was a ruin, flesh hanging in strips from her skull. Empty eye sockets stared at me accusingly as her mouth opened in a silent scream.

"No," I whispered, backing away. "You're not real. You can't be."

Mary's spectral form drifted closer, her ruined hands reaching for me. I turned to flee, only to find my path blocked by more ghostly figures. The faces of all the women who had died, murdered by Arthur—Elizabeth Stride, Catherine Eddowes, and others whose names I couldn't recall. All staring at me with hollow eyes full of accusation.

"I didn't kill you," I pleaded, though my words rang hollow even to my own ears. "It was Arthur. He's the one behind all of this."

The spectral women closed in around me, their cold hands grasping at my clothes. I could feel their touch now, icy fingers digging into my flesh. The world spun around me as their silent screams filled my head.

I collapsed to my knees, overwhelmed by the onslaught of accusing spirits. Their cold touch seeped into my bones, chilling me to my very core. I wanted to scream, to run, but my body refused to obey.

"Please," I begged, my voice barely a whisper. "I'm trying to stop this. To save you all."

But the specters paid no heed to my pleas. Their ethereal forms pressed closer, suffocating me with the stench of decay and the weight of their collective anguish.

"Why are you letting them kill us, Jack?" they echoed.

"Please, please. I'm trying! Give me time! I'm trying! The veil! Arthur, he's doing all of this!" I begged.

Their voices echoed in my mind, a cacophony of pain and accusation. I closed my eyes, trying to shut out the horrific visions, but they persisted behind my eyelids. The weight of their collective suffering pressed down on me, threatening to crush me beneath its enormity.

"I'm sorry," I whispered, my voice breaking. "I'm so sorry."

Suddenly, a new voice cut through the chaos, smooth, familiar, and terrifyingly real.

"Now, now, ladies. I believe you've tormented our dear Jack enough for one night."

My eyes snapped open to see a wraith standing, or rather, floating in front of me. The spectral women faded at its presence, their anguished cries diminishing to whispers on the wind.

My tear-stained eyes strained to focus on the figure before me, shifting and fluctuating like a mirage in the desert. Its very presence sent shivers down my spine, as if I were staring into the maw of some unfathomable nightmare.

"What are you?" I croaked, my voice trembling with fear and confusion. "What have you done to me?"

The creature smiled, its grin wide and sharp like knives glinting in the moonlight. "Oh dear Jack," it purred, its voice dripping with malice. "I am Morgana, and what I have done is simply reveal the true nature of our reality."

I recoiled as she pointed at her long nails, a twisted smirk crossing her face. "The Veil has been lifted," she continued, her voice filled with sick delight. "And now you see the world for what it truly is—chaotic, unpredictable, and utterly terrifying."

Struggling to stand, my mind spinning with disbelief and terror, I could only manage a weak denial. "No... this can't be real."

Morgana's laughter echoed through the empty street, each cackle sending chills down my spine. "Real? My dear Jack," she sneered, stepping closer until her sulfuric stench filled my nostrils. "Death is merely a construct. These 'murders' that plague your city are just steps in a grand plan."

I shook my head frantically, trying to comprehend her words through the fog of dread that consumed me. "I want no part in this madness," I spat, feeling bile rise in my throat.

But Morgana's smile only widened, revealing rows upon rows of razor-sharp teeth that seemed to multiply with each passing second. "Oh, but you already are," she whispered seductively, her form shifting between ghostly and solid. "You are our perfect patsy, dear Jack. You have played your role perfectly, even if you were unaware of it."

Her words struck me like a blow to the stomach, stealing my breath and leaving me reeling. "No," I gasped, stumbling back in horror. "I won't let you frame an innocent man."

But Morgana's laughter only grew louder, reverberating through the deserted street and filling my ears with a cacophony of madness. "Innocent?" she sneered, her form flickering in and out of existence. "You are our willing participant in this grand scheme. Every move you've made has been part of our plan. Whether you want to admit it or not."

"You're lying," I hissed, refusing to believe her twisted version of reality. "I would never willingly be a part of something like this."

Morgana's laughter died down and she fixed me with a cold stare. "Believe what you will, Jack," she said calmly. "But deep down you know the truth."

I shook my head defiantly, refusing to give in to her manipulations. Suddenly, an idea struck me—if Morgana was real and capable of such feats, perhaps there was a way to stop her and put an end to this chaos once and for all.

With newfound determination, I looked up at her with steely resolve. "If what you say is true," I said through gritted teeth. "Then I'll find a way to stop you."

Morgana's wicked grin widened and she let out a cruel laugh. "Oh dear Jack," she cooed mockingly. "You can't stop us. We are beyond your comprehension."

But I refused to back down, my fear replaced by anger and determination. With every ounce of courage I could muster, I took a step forward towards Morgana and declared: "I won't let innocent people die because of your sick games."

And with that, Morgana's form flickered one last time before disappearing completely, leaving me standing alone in the dark, determined to put an end to her and her twisted games with Arthur.

Chapter Four
The Ritual

I stumbled back to my home, clutching my chest in agony. The icy tendrils of the women's tortured souls still lingered on my skin, their screams echoing in my mind like a never-ending nightmare. "How could they do this?" I thought as I fumbled with the lock on my door. Every nerve in my body was on edge, expecting those spectral fingers to reach out and drag me into the abyss.

With a shuddering breath, I stepped inside and slammed the door shut behind me, but the silence in my empty flat was deafening. I reached for a match, my trembling hands barely able to strike it. As the faint flame flickered to life, I caught a glimpse of my reflection in the hallway mirror, my face was ashen, eyes wild with terror.

But it wasn't just my own face that stared back at me. In the mirror, I saw the contorted faces of those women, forever trapped in eternal agony. Their screams grew louder as they clawed at me from within the glass,

I stumbled back, frantically reaching for a bottle of whiskey to calm my nerves. But as I poured myself a drink, I noticed a dark stain spreading across my shirt. Blood? No, something far worse—a viscous, black ichor that seemed to pulsate with malevolent life.

In a panic, I tore off my jacket only to see more of the cursed substance covering my skin. Suddenly, there came a soft scratching sound from the window and when I turned to look, there was a pallid face with hollow eyes pressed against the pane, smiling with razor-sharp teeth.

Before I could react, it vanished. But the scratching continued, now coming from within the walls themselves. In desperation, I grabbed a pen and ink and began writing. "They're coming." I scrawled frantically. "I will stop them. I swear on it."

But as I wrote, the ink spilled across my desk like a dark omen. It formed intricate patterns that seemed to writhe with a life of their own, and for a moment, I saw faces within its depths, their mouths stretched wide in silent screams.

Then, with a gust of wind, my candle was extinguished, leaving me alone in the darkness with only the frantic scratching sounds surrounding me. In a panic, I stumbled backwards and fell to the floor, feeling as if the very darkness itself was pressing down on me.

But it wasn't just an oppressive force—it was alive. The black ichor had spread further, seeping into my skin and rooting me to the spot. And then, from within the rippling mirror on the wall, a hand emerged—pale, skeletal, reaching for me with grasping fingers.

I tried to stand and flee, but my legs refused to move. The darkness had consumed me entirely now, and as the hand drew closer, I felt my sanity slipping away. The last thing I saw before everything went black was my own reflection in the mirror, grinning back at me with those same needle-sharp teeth.

I awoke with a start, my heart pounding in my chest. The room was pitch black, save for a sliver of moonlight creeping through the curtains. I fumbled for a match, desperate to banish the shadows that seemed to writhe and twist in the corners of my vision.

As the flame sputtered to life, I saw that my desk was pristine, no sign of the spilled ink or frantic scribbles. Had it all been a nightmare? But the lingering chill on my skin and the faint echo of screams in my mind told me otherwise.

I rose on unsteady legs, my body aching as if I'd been in a brawl. Every step sent shockwaves of pain through my limbs. As I made my way to the washbasin, I caught sight of my reflection in the mirror. My face was gaunt, eyes sunken and haunted. But it was the dark stain on my collar that made my blood run cold.

With trembling fingers, I unbuttoned my shirt. There, etched into my flesh like a blasphemous tattoo, was a symbol I recognized from the occult tomes I'd been studying. It pulsed with an unholy light, and I knew with sickening certainty that I had been marked.

A soft tapping at the window made me whirl around. There, pressed against the glass, was a raven. Its eyes gleamed with an intelligence that was anything but natural. In its beak was a scrap of paper.

I hesitated, every instinct screaming at me to flee. But I knew I was already too deeply entangled in this web of darkness. With a deep breath, I opened the window and took the paper from the bird's beak.

As I unfolded it, the raven cawed once and took flight, disappearing into the night. The note contained just five words, written in a spidery hand:

"The ritual begins at midnight."

I crumpled the note in my fist, a cold sweat breaking out across my brow. Midnight. I glanced at the clock on the mantle, it was already half past eleven. My mind raced, torn between the urge to barricade myself in my rooms and the gnawing certainty that I had to act.

With trembling hands, I donned my coat and hat, stuffing a revolver into my pocket. The weight of it was reassuring, though I doubted its efficacy against the horrors I'd witnessed. As I stepped out into the foggy London night, the gas lamps cast eerie halos in the mist.

I knew where I had to go. The abandoned church on the outskirts of Whitechapel had been at the center of my investigations. Its decrepit spire loomed like an accusing finger pointed at the heavens.

As I approached, I heard a low chanting emanating from within. The sound sent shivers down my spine, an otherworldly chorus that seemed to vibrate in my very bones. The symbol on my chest burned in response, as if awakening to some unholy summons.

I crept towards a broken window, peering inside.

forward, eyes like voids beneath their hoods. I was trapped in a nightmarish tableau; brutality woven with shadows danced at the fringes of my vision, a twisted ballet orchestrated by an unseen conductor. "No escape!" echoed their taunts, harmonizing with the relentless rhythm of my thundering heart.

I reeled against a wall, desperately trying to gather what remained of my fraying sanity. The symbol's glow intensified, illuminating grotesque carvings on crumbling bricks—ancient depictions of sacrifice and torment that seemed to study me with knowing disdain. "What do you want from me?" I screamed at the abyss before me, voice cracking under the weight of despair.

The masked figure stepped closer, dagger glinting under flickering light like a wicked star. His voice dripped honeyed malice, "You think you possess free will? How quaint." He waved his hand toward the altar. "This, this is our final victim. Before your downfall."

Chapter Five
Fractures

Mary Jane Kelly lay strapped to the altar, screaming and gagged.

The sight of her—bound, trembling, the shroud of innocence stripped away—sent a frigid spike through my heart. Her eyes, wide with terror, begged for salvation that I was ill-equipped to provide. A desperate scream clawed at my throat, but the laughter from the cultists drowned it out, a cacophony of delight at my impending failure. I stumbled forward instinctively, but those spectral figures closed ranks, their presence suffocating as they towered over me.

"Fool," the masked leader taunted, dagger poised above the altar like an ominous pendulum. "You think you can save her? You're bereft of strength and riddled with madness." His voice bore a chilling sweetness, each word curling like smoke in the surrounding air.

"No!" I gasped, desperation pouring forth as I struggled against the overwhelming tide of dread. In that moment, clarity pierced through the fog of fear—a glimpse of the truth hidden beneath layers of manipulation and shadows. "Your rituals... they don't bind me! I am not your pawn!" Each word struck like hammer blows against the soft iron of despair that had wrapped itself around my resolve.

With renewed fervor, I raised my weapon again; this time it felt heavier in my grasp yet somehow lighter in spirit. "Let her go!"

The leader merely chuckled darkly, an echo of amusement cascading from his lips. "You think defiance will shatter our bonds? How naive." He gestured to Mary Jane, whose eyes fluttered in frantic hope despite her bindings. "She is but an offering. A spark to..."

"Stop!" I exclaimed cutting him off, my voice hoarse and hollow. The cultists paused for merely a heartbeat, their hoods shifting slightly as they regarded me with scornful amusement. "You can't do this!" It sounded feeble even to my ears, a mere echo against the cacophony of their laughter.

The masked leader leaned closer, his dagger poised like a serpent ready to strike. "Why not? You think you can save her? The ritual demands her. Her very essence is what we crave to complete the gate."

My heart splintered at the utterance of her name. I couldn't let this happen. Rage surged through me—hot and frantic—a desperate surge of adrenaline that threatened to drown out my dread. "Release her!" I yelled, desperation turning into fury, a roaring tempest within me.

But the figures only laughed again, an abhorrent symphony that echoed around the stone room like the harbinger of death itself. Their mirth twisted in my gut as I struggled against the burgeoning terror—a potent reminder of my own helplessness.

"Fool," sneered another hooded shadow. The dagger glimmered as he twisted it between bony fingers.

A shiver snaked up my spine as their laughter crested like a wave, and for an instant, the chamber's shadows seemed to thicken. The air grew heavy with the scent of incense and blood, a vile concoction that mingled with the dampness of the stone walls. I could feel the walls closing in, pressing against me before everything went black.

I awoke several days later on Dorset street. The cobblestones beneath me were slick with rain, glistening like the scales of some slumbering beast. I pushed myself upright, the weight of memory flooding in like a tide of ice. *Mary Jane.* A whisper of her name clung to the air, a haunting echo that twisted my insides. My heart raced, each thump a cruel reminder of my failure. I had been cast aside, discarded by powers that laughed at the fragility of hope.

As I rose, shadows flickered at the periphery of my vision—figures darting just beyond the reach of light. My breath quickened; the night was cloaked in malevolence, and I felt it coiling around me like a serpent waiting to strike.

"Your fears are my playthings," I imagined Morgana whispering from the depths of my mind, her voice coiling around my spine like a chilling caress.

The street lay empty, save for the distant wail of sirens and the low murmur of despair that wafted through the night air. The gas lamps sputtered above, their flickering flames casting grotesque shadows upon crumbling brick walls—monsters writhing in agony against their constraints. I staggered forward, longing for answers but tethered by uncertainty.

Footsteps echoed behind me, heavy and deliberate; they drew nearer with each beat of my heart. Panic clawed at my throat as I turned to confront whatever specter pursued me. But there was nothing—only darkness nibbling at the edges of reality as it sought to envelop me whole. A rustle sounded from deeper within the alleyway—a movement, a scurry. I paced forward to find a body. Mary Jane Kelly, slain. I looked down, my hands coated in blood.

I staggered back, the world spinning in grotesque distortion. The body lay before me, marred by violence, a macabre testament to what had transpired. A cold numbness seeped into my bones, mingling with the bitter taste of regret on my tongue. "No," I breathed, the word barely escaping my cracked lips. "This cannot be..."

Yet there she was, Mary Jane, her delicate features twisted and pale as death had claimed her. The street seemed to close in tighter, the oppressive weight of sorrow pressing against my chest like a vice. My mind spiraled into chaos, grasping futilely at strands of sanity as they frayed.

I dropped to my knees beside her, trembling fingers brushing against lifeless skin. "I failed you," I murmured through clenched teeth, the confession laced with sharp edges of despair.

From the depths of those suffocating shadows, Morgana's laughter unfurled—a haunting melody that danced mockingly around me. It echoed off the cobblestones and swirled like a tempest through the alleys of my mind.

"Your failure is exquisite," she cooed, her voice dripping with dark delight. "Each drop of blood cries your name; it calls for vengeance."

"Leave me!" I yelled into the void, knowing full well that she would do no such thing. This was her domain, and I was merely a puppet strung along by invisible threads of dread. But deep down, tangled within my despair, an ember of defiance ignited—a flicker of resistance to her malevolence.

"Run," she whispered softly. "They're coming."

I heard the distant wail of whistles from the encroaching police. How long have I been here? Covered in her blood? Surely they'll know I didn't do this!

Yet, the shadows whispered differently. In that moment, I felt them congeal around me, coiling like serpents, wrapping my thoughts in a cold embrace that stifled reason.

"You will be their prime suspect," Morgana purred,

the cadence of her voice weaving through my panic like a silken thread.

"They'll find you here—guilty as sin." Arthur's voice joined in.

I stood abruptly, the cobblestones slick beneath my knees, and staggered back into the depths of the alley. My breath came quicker, each inhale a shuddering gasp at the thought of being ensnared by blue coats wielding pikes, their accusing gazes piercing through the fog of my guilt. I could already hear distant shouts mingling with the cries of the night; they would come for me soon.

"Flee, little lamb," Morgana crooned from her unseen throne somewhere beyond sight.

"But where can you run? The city is rife with your failure," Arthur continued, their voices morphing into one.

As if summoned by their words, darkness seeped from every crack and crevice, twisting itself into grotesque forms that taunted my escape. I pressed my back against the damp brick wall, fingers digging deep into the mortar as I fought against despair creeping over me like ivy. Shadows flickered again at the corner of my eye—faces deformed and twisted in horrific delight.

"Go on!" they urged, their voices a seductive balm laced with venom. "Let them chase you through their own nightmare."

With trembling resolve, I turned and plunged deeper into the alley's maw—a narrow corridor that swallowed hopes whole and spat forth only anguish. My footsteps pounding against the slick cobblestones. I'm almost there.

Almost, I can feel them closing in. The shadows? Or is it the police? I need to run, run, run faster! FASTER! Faster!

I raced into the oppressive embrace of the alley, where the dim moonlight barely penetrated the suffocating darkness. Each footfall echoed like a drumbeat heralding my doom, reverberating against the walls as if announcing my hopes of escape to those who would drag me back into despair. The air was thick with dread, a palpable miasma, and I could feel it clawing at my lungs, choking the very breath from my throat.

"Run, little lamb," Morgana echoed, her voice curling around me like smoke from an extinguished candle. "You think you can escape your sins? They will find you. They will always find you."

With each step, the shadows morphed into nameless horrors. I could hear their whispering laughter—a chorus of taunts woven with malicious delight that thrummed beneath my skin. I pressed onward, heart racing in a frantic dance of survival, but doubt slithered through my thoughts like poison. What if they were right? What if this dark labyrinth led only to more despair?

I turned a corner sharply and stumbled into a broader street that glistened wetly under the gas lamps' sickly glow. The night air crackled with tension as my gaze whipped around for any sign of salvation or pursuers. But there was only silence hanging heavy in the dampness, as if the city itself held its breath in anticipation of what would unfold next.

Then I heard it. A distant yet familiar sound cutting

through the stillness, the rhythmic clattering of boots on cobblestones, drawing nearer with each second. Panic surged anew within me; they were coming—hunters eager for the kill.

"Stop!" they yelled, but I couldn't. I was a scapegoat, a patsy! They would never believe the true evils that lay just beneath their feet. Beyond their minds eye. Lurking, waiting for the opportunity to feast on human folly.

My heart pounded, a wild thing desperate for freedom, as I darted into a narrow passage flanked by crumbling edifices. The walls closed in, suffocating me with their encroaching shadows, and the wet scent of decay lingered in the air. I pressed my back against the cool stone, half-hidden from view, and held my breath— hoping, praying that some divine serendipity would spare me from their grasp.

Yet, as I crouched there, shrouded in darkness, a voice pierced through the din of my racing thoughts like a razor's edge.

"You think this will save you?"

It was Arthur, materializing from the very shadows themselves with an ethereal poise that sent icy fingers dancing along my spine. His tailored suit clung to him like a second skin—sickly immaculate in the depths of this horror. "Hiding only prolongs your suffering," he continued, his blue eyes glistening with malevolent insight.

"Why do you haunt me?" I spat through clenched teeth, each word a defiance against the dread that clung to me. "You are as much a part of this nightmare as Morgana!"

Arthur's lips twisted into an unsettling smile that held no warmth—a prelude to torment.

"Such a clever little rabbit," Morgana sang softly above me, her presence suffocating yet intoxicating. "You've entered their maze with no exit in sight, and still you think you can outsmart them?"

I stumbled back, nausea twisting in my gut. "Get away from me! Leave me be!" I spat, feeling absurdly exposed under his calculating gaze.

"Hmm, Jack, how poetic," he murmured, that infuriating calmness never wavering. "Yet here we stand, and it is you who bears the weight of accusation upon your shoulders. They will judge you for the sins you claim are not yours. But tell me," he leaned closer, his breath a frigid whisper against my ear, "do you truly believe you are innocent?"

The air thickened, pressing against my chest with every word he spoke, suffocating reason and igniting a wildfire of dread. I tried to turn away, to shut him out, but the shadows clung to me like a shroud, dragging forth memories that clawed at the edges of my mind. "Innocent? No... but it was never me!" I shouted, desperation twisting my tone into something almost unrecognizable.

Arthur's laughter echoed in the narrow passage, a chilling sound that slithered into the depths of my soul. "Ah, but who else could be held accountable for such delightful chaos? They will paint you as the villain, Jack —a madman lurking in the alleyways, a specter of depravity." His words wrapped around me like chain links, binding tighter with each syllable. "And what will you do when they come for you? Will you embrace your fate or fight against it?"

I sank to my knees, fingers curling into filthy cobblestones as the wretched reality pressed upon me. They would accuse me—oh yes! Every victim's blood would stain my hands in their eyes. But deep within, buried beneath layers of shame and fear, a flicker of defiance ignited. "I refuse to be their puppet!" I snarled, desperation lending strength to my voice. "I will not dance to your tune!"

"Such rebellion," Morgana's voice dripped with mockery from the darkness above, her form coalescing just beyond sight. "But tell me... How long can one fight against the inevitable?"

I raised my head defiantly. "Long enough to prove I had no hand in this depravity."

& SON

Chapter Six
Depravity

The days and nights melted together, each one a hazy blur of darkness and paranoia. The sigil, that cursed mark seared into my skin, throbbed like a living thing, pulsing with malicious intent. I pressed myself against the cold stone walls of the abandoned building, seeking solace in their unforgiving embrace.

The shadows whispered to me, taunting and tempting me with secrets and promises. My fractured mind struggled to resist their influence, but it was a losing battle. They had chosen me as their vessel, their pawn in this twisted game of power and control.

"It was them," I hissed through clenched teeth, my voice cracking with madness. "They did this to me. Made me... made me..." My fingers trembled as they traced over the twisted sigil on my flesh, feeling its malevolent energy coursing through my veins.

Footsteps echoed in the distance, coming closer and

closer. Was it the authorities or some other dark force sent to hunt me down? It didn't matter—they were all out to get me now. A sickening mix of terror and anger welled up inside me as I sank to my knees, unable to escape the inevitable accusations and punishment that awaited me.

But deep within, buried under layers of fear and desperation, a spark of defiance ignited. "I refuse to be your plaything!" I screamed into the night, defying both my physical and mental captors. "I will not succumb to your twisted desires!" The shadows recoiled in fury at my resistance, but I knew deep down that it was only a matter of time before they would claim me completely.

The footsteps grew louder, a grim sonata of dread that accompanied my rising panic. My heart, that traitorous organ, thundered in my chest as though it sought to shatter my ribcage and escape into the cavernous night. I pressed my back harder against the stone, its chill seeping through my clothing like ice water into my bones. Each breath came ragged and shallow, an agonizing reminder of my fragility.

The shadows stirred, swirling around me with impatient glee, eager to witness my undoing. With every heartbeat, they closed in tighter, their whispers growing more insistent, more alluring.

"Join us," they beckoned, their voices slick as oil. "Let go of this futile struggle."

I gritted my teeth, clenching fists stained with the grime of guilt. The innocent faces of those I had failed flickered in my mind's eye—each one a specter of their own demise. Their haunting gazes bore into me, tauntingly forgiving yet filled with the unspoken accusation that hung heavy in the air: *You let them die.*

A flicker of movement caught my attention; a shadow detached itself from the mass and approached me with a languid grace. I squinted against the pervasive gloom, desperate to decipher the figure's intent. It was neither predator nor prey but something far more sinister, something familiar yet devilishly transformed.

"Jack," it cooed in a voice that licked at my sanity like flames at kindling. "Oh dear, Jack... Do you not remember me?" Pale hands extended toward me, fingers splayed as if to capture what remained of my soul.

Recognition clawed at the recesses of my memory—a long-forgotten face who had slipped between the cracks of time and despair. But this creature wore their skin like a mask, stretched taut over grotesque truths hidden just beneath the surface.

"You should have listened," it sang sweetly, the smile curving like a razor's edge.

The footsteps halted. Breathless anticipation crackled in the air as if the very shadows conspired against me. I could feel eyes upon me; unseen judges poised to render their verdict on a life marred by choices made and forsaken.

"Will you join us?" the figure whispered again, it's voice a slow serenade entwining with my thoughts, each syllable chipping away at my resolve until nothing remained but the echo of despair.

In that moment, as madness and clarity tightened their grip on my mind, I realized, there was but one way to silence it—the truth. It would either free me or devour me whole. And so I drew myself up from the cold embrace of stone, facing this wraith-like apparition born from regret and longing.

"I choose neither." My voice rang through the dark like a bell tolling for the damned. "I will carve out my own fate."

As the first rays of dawn threatened to break through the dark, I stood before the creature with a sense of defiance. The shadows recoiled from my determination, but in that brief moment of strength, I could feel a glimmer of hope. A spark that even they couldn't snuff out. But as the police whistles grew closer, I knew my time was running out. They would have to listen to me, they would have to see the truth.

But then her laughter filled the air, cold and cruel. Morgana, her spirit lingering in the corners of my mind, taunting and tormenting me with every step. She reveled in my fear, feeding off it like a malignant parasite.

"You think you can escape me?" Her voice was a silky thread of menace that slithered around my thoughts. "You are bound to this darkness just as tightly as flesh clings to bone."

The creature before me shifted and twisted, revealing itself to be Morgana herself, her eyes gleaming with wicked delight. The shadows swirled around her like obedient servants, caressing her form with an other-worldly grace.

"I watched you struggle in your pathetic existence," she hissed, her words dripping with venom. "Each desperate act dragging you deeper into my grasp. You are the very embodiment of all that is vile and wretched."

I wanted to deny her words, to scream out in defiance, but my voice failed me. Doubt gnawed at my resolve, whispering that perhaps she was right. That I was just another monster hiding in plain sight. "No... this is not who I am," I protested weakly, though even I could hear the uncertainty in my own voice.

Morgana sighed dramatically, a look of mock sorrow on her face. "Truth is an illusion in this world we inhabit," she mused, twirling a strand of her hair between her fingers. "You may reject it now, but like shadows that linger long after the light fades, so too will your guilt cling to you." Her laughter was a chilling symphony that echoed around us, drowning out any hope or reason I had left.

I could feel the weight of my failures crushing me, suffocating me with every breath. How many lives had been lost because of my inaction? The faces of my victims swirled in my mind like a never-ending nightmare, their blood staining my hands and soul. But even as I drowned in this sea of despair, a flicker of determination sparked within me.

"I will make them listen!" I shouted into the void that separated us. The police were close; if I could just prove them wrong, expose Morgana's deceit...

Her eyes narrowed, a feral glint shining through the emerald depths. "Such an intriguing notion," she purred, circling me like a predator toying with its prey. "To play the hero when all you've ever done is kill. Kill, and kill, and kill." She leaned in close, her voice dripping with malice. "But what if they already know?"

My heart sank at her words, doubts creeping back in like venomous snakes coiling around my resolve. What if I wasn't meant to be their savior? What if I was always meant to be their monster?

With each passing second that brought me closer to my inevitable fate, Morgana's form began to shift and change once more, morphing into someone else entirely. Arthur. They both circled around me, mocking and prodding at my sanity until it threatened to snap under the pressure. But deep down, somewhere in the depths of my shattered mind, I knew one thing for certain: I was not a killer.

Yet the world around me convulsed, twisting like a grotesque marionette at the hands of my tormentors. Arthur's presence was a cloak of ice, slipping over me, as he emerged from the shadows with a smile that sliced through the night.

"Ah, Jack," he purred, his voice smooth as silk yet laced with venom. "What a tragic little play we've found ourselves in. You seek absolution from those who will only see you as the monster you've become."

I flinched at his words, feeling the weight of their truth pressing like iron chains upon my chest. Morgana's laughter danced around us, an eerie harmony to Arthur's chilling serenade.

"Why fight against what you are?" she crooned, her fingers weaving through the air like tendrils of smoke.

"Embrace it! Revel in your nature! You have touched the void; now let it consume you."

"Shut up!" I cried out, desperation clawing at my throat. The police whistles grew louder, echoing like a death knell for my sanity. I could feel their approach—bright lanterns slicing through the fog of my despair—illuminating my sins with every step they took toward me.

"Do you hear that?" Arthur taunted, tilting his head as if savoring the distant cacophony of chaos. "They come for you, Jack. But tell me," he leaned closer, breath hot against my ear, "what do they really want? A murderer to punish? Or perhaps, a sacrificial lamb to sate their insatiable hunger for blood?"

I fought back tears, staring into his piercing blue eyes that seemed to read my soul as easily as one might read a child's storybook.

"You don't understand!" I shouted in defiance. "I am not what they say! I refuse to be their pawn!"

Morgana stepped forward again, an ethereal figure wreathed in shadows. "But you are already ensnared," she whispered softly, her voice curling around me like frost on a winter's eve. "You've danced to our tune all along."

As their words sank deeper into my mind like poison, each syllable dragging me further down into the abyss, I felt reality begin to warp around me. The air thickened with dread; it was palpable and suffocating. Each breath tasted metallic and bitter as visions flickered before my eyes—bloodied bodies sprawled on cobblestones, haunting wails echoing through desolate streets, and whispers in alleys that chanted my name like an unholy hymn.

"No!" I screamed, but it sounded hollow even to me —an echo ricocheting off an unseen wall of despair. "I won't succumb! I can't!"

Arthur and Morgana exchanged glances filled with cruel amusement, a silent agreement passing between them that sealed my fate further still.

"Then fight," Arthur encouraged gleefully, stepping back and spreading his arms wide like a maestro conducting an unseen orchestra. "Fight against yourself! But know this: We are always here... lurking in the recesses of your darkened heart."

And then I felt it, a shift within myself, a splitting sensation as if two halves were being forcibly torn apart as the constables closed in.

"I'm not what you think," I yelled to them. "I am tainted by the machinations of others!" As they closed in, clubs at the ready, everything went black.

Awakening was like breaking the surface of a black, viscous sea—every inch propelled by the weight of dread. My surroundings materialized slowly, darkness receding to reveal a dimly lit room, its walls adorned with peeling wallpaper that seemed to weep with the ghosts of the past. Shadows clung to every corner, earnest in their pursuit to swallow me whole.

The stench of decay curled around my nostrils, and I pushed myself upright, the floorboards groaning beneath me like tortured souls. They were here—watching. I could feel their eyes pressing against my flesh, hungry and malevolent. I turned sharply in every direction, half-expecting to see Arthur's sneer or Morgana's chilling visage lurking just beyond my sight. Yet all that greeted me was suffocating silence.

"Am I dead?" I murmured, voice trembling as it cut through the thick air. The room offered no answer—only an oppressive stillness that threatened to crush me as surely as any blade would. Shadows flickered at the edges of my vision, teasing me with glimpses of something unsettling beyond perception.

My fingers brushed against a familiar object—a tattered journal, its pages stained and frayed, like memories clawing their way into existence. The ink within twisted and writhed upon the pages, spelling out secrets best left forgotten. "What have I done?" I whispered hoarsely, haunted by the echoes of laughter that spiraled up from the depths of my mind.

The frantic scratching of my pen filled the air as I scribbled feverishly—words tumbling forth like trapped spirits escaping from their prison: *They are not mine; they belong to the shadows.* Yet as quickly as clarity arrived, it slipped through my fingers like blood running from an open wound.

"Do they come for you now? Or do they come for your spirit?" That voice again—cold as winter's breath, entwined with a melody that resonated deep within my fractured psyche. Morgana emerged from the darkness like smoke rising from a dying ember, her eyes glowing with malicious delight. "Your struggle is entertainment for us both."

I gritted my teeth against her presence, summoning whatever remnants of resolve still dwelled inside me. "Get away from me!" My words were sharp shards of ice thrown into her inferno, but they barely scratched the surface.

"Why resist?" she purred, gliding closer until her wraith-like form hovered mere inches from mine. "You cannot escape what you are." In her gaze lay an overwhelming certainty, an affirmation that gnawed at my insides like a festering wound refusing to heal.

"I'm not a monster," I croaked back with unsteady conviction, even as her laughter reverberated around me like an unholy chant.

With each heartbeat came a drumroll leading to a crescendo of madness—a tempest raging just beneath the skin. My own thoughts betrayed me; they spiraled into darkness and despair until whispers echoed louder than screams: *You are one of them; you are one of them.*

"Oi, you in there! Be quiet before you disturb the other prisoners!" a voice called out, thick and demanding.

"I... I don't... What are you saying? Where am I?" I called into the darkness.

"You're in the slammer, Ripper."

Chapter Seven
Baton

The words echoed like a death sentence, the very sound of them slicing through me like a sharpened blade. Ripper—a name stained with blood and terror, a title that had been thrust upon me against my will, branding me as a monster in the eyes of the world. In this grim cell, surrounded by the ghosts of my past sins, I was nothing but a ghost myself—a phantom haunting the depths of this condemned prison.

"Ripper," I repeated in disbelief, my own voice betraying me as it trembled with fear and denial. "I am not—"

"Not what?" the voice taunted, its owner stepping out of the shadows to reveal a figure cloaked in darkness and despair—a living embodiment of this hellish place. "A murderer? A fiend? You were at every crime scene, lapping up the blood like a hound on the hunt. Sounds like the Ripper to me." A deep chuckle rumbled through the air, dripping with scorn and contempt.

I pressed my hands against my temples, trying to hold onto reality as it slipped through my fingers like sand. Whispers swirled and clashed within my mind—a chorus of voices accusing and pleading all at once. "They're wrong!" I shouted, desperation taking hold like a vice around my heart. "You don't understand! I am innocent!"

"Innocent?" The figure drew closer, looming over me with an aura of menace that seemed to suffocate even the dim light in this dank cell. "You are trapped here now, my friend. Innocence is a luxury you can no longer afford."

And then the laughter rose again, a sweet, mocking sound that made my skin crawl. "Oh, how delightful! They shall see you for what you truly are—the architect of your own downfall!" Her voice was like a siren's call, luring me further into madness.

"No!" I snapped back at her, clinging desperately to the journal in my hands—my only tether to reality in this realm of nightmares. "Your words are poison! Twisting the truth!" But as I looked down at the pages filled with confessions too terrible to face, each word seemed to dance and taunt me "Crimson rivers flow and shadows linger where life once breathed." The journal held a mirror up to my soul, revealing the darkness within.

"Can you not hear them?" I pleaded with the guard. "The true killers are here with us, in this very cell!"

A loud clang echoed through the bars, shattering my fragile grip on reality. "Madman, be silent. I grow tired of your ravings," he sneered.

"How can you be so calm?" I seethed, rage igniting within me like a bonfire. "I am an innocent man."

"Silence!" he bellowed, his baton striking the bars once more. "I will not ask again, Ripper."

The guard's ferocity died down to an uneasy quiet, leaving me alone with the weight of his disdain. My heart thudded against my ribs like a caged animal, desperate to escape the confines of this nightmare. The shadows curled around me, eager to swallow my sanity whole.

"Can you not feel it?" I rasped, the words escaping my lips like a prayer cast into the abyss. "The air is thick with their presence, their malice lingering like smoke after a fire." I stood abruptly, driven by a grim urgency to reveal my tormentor's truth. "They are here! They dwell in the corners of this cursed cell, waiting to consume me!"

A guttural snort was the only reply he afforded me. Such contempt from one who wore ignorance like a cloak! He could not know what roamed these haunted halls. He had not witnessed the unholy communion of shadows and whispers that plagued my nights.

"Listen to me!" I shouted into the void, my words swallowed by the stillness, as if the very walls conspired against me. "I am not your monster! I am merely a vessel for their darkness."

Unseen eyes watched from the corners of the cell, whispering secrets that fed on my torment. Each creak of the decrepit structure sent tremors through my sanity, urging me to question what was real and what was mere illusion spun by a deranged mind.

The guard turned, his teeth sharp, rows upon rows of them with eyes dark as pitch. "You, are the monster, Ripper. Everyone knows it."

I staggered back on my feet, back against the cold wall. Desperate to escape his glare, the icy tendrils of his soul reaching to me. "Stop! Stop!" I screamed.

But my cries fell silent, swallowed by the void that feasted on despair. The guard, a grotesque marionette of malice, drew closer still, his breath an icy fog that wrapped around my throat. I turned my head from him, unwilling to behold the monstrosity masquerading as a man. Instead, I sought solace in the journal clasped tightly in my trembling hands, its pages now a cacophony of truths and lies entwined.

"Cry all you wish," the guard hissed, his voice a slithering serpent in my ear. "It will not save you from your fate. You, are a killer. Jack."

The shadows stretched and twisted like grotesque limbs, pulling me deeper into their embrace. I could feel them whispering now—voices entwined with my thoughts, weaving a tapestry of horrors long buried beneath the weight of dread. They sang of my sins, each note resonating with a truth so vile it threatened to claw its way to the surface.

"No!" I shrieked again, though the fire within me waned, each word drained like blood from a wound sustained too long. "I am not their puppet! Stop!"

The guard watched from his post with an expression carved from stone. He had become merely an observer in this macabre drama unfolding in my cell—a man mired in duty yet oblivious to the nightmares skirmishing just beyond his reach.

And just then, a flicker in the room's oppressive

gloom caught my eye. A shadow detached itself from the corner like a nightmarish sentinel, an apparition rising from forgotten depths. Its features blurred and indistinct yet unmistakably anguished. I recognized it: It was Mary —the first of many who'd breathed their last under my horrid watch.

A chill enveloped me, a creeping dread that coiled tighter than ever around my chest. "Forgive me! I couldn't save you," I rasped towards her spectral form, reaching out as if to grasp something more substantial than the mere air swirling about us. But she merely hovered there, her ghostly visage twisting into a mockery of sorrow.

"Forgiven?" her voice echoed hollowly through the prison walls. "You know not what you ask for! You wear their guilt as your flesh, you are wrapped in their despair."

A dizzying vertigo swept over me as memories clawed their way back—distant screams ricocheting off walls painted with shadow and regret—the realization settling heavily upon my shoulders like a shroud woven of anguish and dread.

The guard's laughter rang out, a cruel symphony that pierced the air like ice shattering against stone. "Go on, Ripper. Speak to the phantoms. Perhaps they'll grant you solace," he taunted, his form blurring in and out of focus as if he too were becoming part of the nightmare.

The guard's laughter twisted through the cell, warping the very air, each note carving into my skull like the rasp of a dull blade. His face seemed to contort, warping in and out of the gloom, shifting between man and something far worse. Something monstrous.

I stumbled back against the damp stone, my fingers grasping at the slick, cold wall, desperate for some anchor, some tether to reality. But there was none. Nothing here was real, and everything was too real all at once. The shadows crawled along the floor like the creeping hands of the dead, slithering up my legs, tightening their grip.

"Speak to them," the guard said again, his voice coiling around me like a serpent. "They know you better than you know yourself."

In the corner, Mary's spectral form hovered, her eyes hollow sockets of endless black, gazing at me not with accusation, but with a strange, suffocating indifference. Her pale lips moved, but no sound escaped—just the silent terror of someone caught between life and death, between forgiveness and damnation.

"No," I muttered, shaking my head, though even the movement felt unsteady, as if my body were no longer entirely my own. "I didn't... I couldn't have..."

But the ghosts wouldn't leave. They *never* left.

The shadows writhed around Mary, stretching across the cell, and from them, more figures emerged. One by one, they rose from the darkness, their faces familiar, etched into the deepest corners of my mind—the faces of the women whose deaths I had been blamed for. Annie, Elizabeth, Catherine, Mary... They stood around me now, their forms flickering in and out of existence like the flame of a candle about to be snuffed out.

"Stop," I whispered, backing into the corner of my cell, though I knew there was nowhere to run. "I didn't kill you. I swear, I didn't."

Mary Nichols, her throat a jagged, open wound, took a step forward. Her voice was a whisper that seemed to come from everywhere and nowhere all at once. "You watched me die, Jack. You stood there as the life drained out of me."

My breath hitched, panic clawing at my chest. I wanted to scream, to deny her words, but the image of her body, discarded in the streets like rubbish, flashed through my mind. *Had I stood there?* Was I there that night, lurking in the fog, watching as her blood soaked the cobblestones?

"No," I rasped, clamping my hands over my ears as if that could shut out the voices. "This isn't real. You're not real."

But they didn't stop. The others stepped forward, their hollow eyes locked on me, each one a reminder of the horrors I'd tried so hard to forget.

"You held the knife, Jack," Elizabeth Stride whispered, her voice brittle as old bones. "You sliced through my skin, felt the warmth of my blood on your hands."

"Stop!" I shouted, falling to my knees, pressing my forehead against the cold stone floor. The ground seemed to pulse beneath me, the very walls breathing, closing in, as if the prison itself was alive—an extension of my own guilt.

"I didn't do it," I whispered, my voice breaking. "I didn't..."

"You did," Annie Chapman's ghost whispered. Her body, mutilated beyond recognition, shifted closer, her empty eyes boring into mine. "You always knew it was you."

The cell swirled, reality collapsing under the weight of their accusations. The guard's mocking laugh echoed again, but now it felt distant, as if he were nothing more than a specter himself, another phantom to haunt me.

"I didn't want to," I gasped, clutching at the fabric of my shirt, trying to rip myself out of this nightmare. But the memories—the things I couldn't remember, or didn't *want* to—rose to the surface. Blood. Always blood. So much of it, coating my hands, my clothes, staining the ground beneath me.

Had I killed them? *Had I really done it?*

The ghosts closed in, their forms pressing against me, cold, weightless, yet suffocating. I couldn't breathe. Their touch was icy, like the hands of death itself, and no matter how much I struggled, I couldn't break free.

I screamed—a raw, animalistic sound that echoed through the cell, bouncing off the walls, growing louder and louder until it was a deafening cacophony inside my skull. I slammed my fists against the floor, desperate to wake up, to escape this nightmare. But no matter how hard I tried, the walls closed in tighter, the ghosts pressed closer, their whispers filling my ears.

"Jack," they called, their voices merging into one ghastly chorus. "Jack, the Ripper."

"Ripper, Ripper, Ripper, Ripper."

I gasped for air, my vision blurring as black spots danced before my eyes. My mind felt as though it were splitting in two, reality fracturing like shattered glass.

The ghosts of my past surrounded me, their faces twisted in pain, in horror, in accusation. And in that moment, a part of me wondered—had I ever been innocent? Or had I been the monster they all believed me to be, the monster *I* had tried so hard to deny?

Could you have killed them all and forgotten? The thought slipped into my mind like a blade, sharp and undeniable.

The shadows swirled around me, tightening their grip. I could no longer tell where the cell ended and where my mind began. There was no line anymore—no division between the past and the present, between guilt and innocence, between reality and madness.

"Cry all you wish," the guard hissed, his voice no longer mocking, but a low, sinister growl. "It will not save you from your fate. You, are a killer, Jack."

I shuddered, collapsing fully against the floor. My breath came in short, shallow gasps, my body shaking uncontrollably. The ghosts faded in and out of view, but their voices remained—always there, whispering, taunting, reminding me of what I had done. Or what I *might* have done.

The truth was a slippery thing, slipping through my fingers every time I tried to grasp it. I was Jack the Ripper. Or perhaps I wasn't. I was a man on the hunt for a killer, or maybe I was the killer all along. I was guilty, or I was innocent.

Or perhaps it didn't matter. Perhaps, in the end, we are all guilty of something.

"Jack," Mary's voice cut through the cacophony, her face hovering inches from mine. Her lips didn't move, but her voice echoed all the same. "You cannot escape."

I closed my eyes, sinking into the cold, hard floor, as the shadows closed in around me. There was no escape. Not from this. Not from myself.

The rusted metal door creaked open, echoing through the dimly lit cell and cutting through the suffocating silence like a sharp blade. Heavy footsteps marched towards me, their heavy thuds sending shivers down my spine. A rough hand grasped my collar and yanked me up, my head lolling back as I struggled to focus on the figure before me.

"Time's up," the guard snarled, his face contorting with contempt.

I blinked, trying to shake off the fog in my mind, but it was no use. I was drowning in it now, consumed by the never-ending darkness that seemed to seep into every corner of this cursed place. The ghosts lurked in the shadows, watching me with their hollow eyes, waiting for their chance to torment me once again. They knew. They had always known.

As I was dragged out of the cell, their haunting whispers followed me, taunting me with every step I took.

"Guilty," they whispered. "Guilty."

And at that moment, I couldn't help but wonder if they were right. If everything they said about me was true.

Chapter Eight
The Journal

The guard propelled me down the dank corridor, the stone walls slick with moisture and despair. Each step resonated deep within me, a reminder that I was shackled by my own sins, my own delusions. The flickering gaslights cast trembling shadows that danced grotesquely upon the walls, contorting into shapes that unnerved my already fragile psyche.

"Keep moving, Ripper," the guard growled, a bitter satisfaction lacing his voice. "We don't have all night."

I stumbled forward, caught in a snare of memory and dread. Mary's visage swirled in my mind, like a ghost tethered to the living world. Was she my anchor or my tormentor? I could almost feel her breath on my neck, cold and foreboding, whispering secrets of what had transpired before the darkness fell.

"Where are you taking me?" I croaked, my throat raw from screaming at shadows. The guard's laughter rang out, a cruel sound that reverberated off the cold stones.

"To meet your maker," he replied, his voice dripping with derision. "Or perhaps just to be judged by those who lie in wait. You'll find no salvation here."

The words cut deeper than any blade; they sunk into my skin and twisted within me like thorns in flesh. As I was dragged forward, a chill crept down my spine, an unnerving sensation that crawled beneath my skin as though Morgana herself had returned to weave her sinister magic around me. I could almost hear her whispering—a melody of despair and delight, drowning out the sound of madness that filled my head.

The corridor narrowed as we approached an ominous door—a heavy oak slab reinforced with iron bars, bearing symbols that danced mockingly before my eyes. It loomed like the mouth of some great beast ready to swallow me whole. I felt my heart thunder in my chest, racing against the inevitable.

"Open it," I hissed through gritted teeth. "Let me face whatever it is you have waiting for me."

With a cruel smile curling on his lips, the guard nodded and shoved me forward into the unyielding darkness beyond the door. My feet stumbled over uneven stones as I crossed the threshold, plunging into an abyss thick with dread.

Inside, shadows swirled like restless spirits in a forgotten graveyard. The air hung heavy with the stench of decay—a noxious blend of damp earth and lingering despair that threatened to choke me. Before me stood figures cloaked in darkness, their faces obscured yet radiating an aura of power that sent tremors through my already frail body.

"Welcome," a voice purred from within the blackness, smooth as silk but laced with venom. My eyes strained to find its source amidst the shifting gloom until they settled on a tall figure dressed in fine tailored garments—Arthur himself stood before me, his icy blue gaze penetrating through the darkness.

"Jack," he said with calculated calmness, "you've been summoned to confront your sins."

"Confront?!" I spat back, incredulity bubbling within me. "What do you know of my sins? You think you can judge me? You're nothing but a specter hiding behind your façade of control!"

The corner of Arthur's mouth twitched—a predatory smile that sent chills rippling across my spine as he stepped closer. "Ah, but Jack... the truth is a far more cunning adversary than one might believe." He gestured towards the encroaching shadows that whispered secrets into my ear, the ghosts had followed me here, eager witnesses to whatever twisted fate awaited.

"What do you want from me?" I gasped breathlessly, desperation clawing at my insides.

"Write," he commanded, his voice wrapping around me like a serpent poised to strike. "Allow your pen to bleed the truth—the ink of your madness swirling upon the page. Write your sins upon the page. Show the world the truth. Claim you're a patsy. Claim you deserve redemption."

"Why?" I croaked, searching Arthur's cold eyes for some semblance of understanding.

A flicker of amusement crossed his face. "Madness is a powerful muse, Jack. It births creativity where clarity fails. Your words will cascade through shadows and awaken dormant echoes. We will weave a tapestry. A dark, exquisite fabric that reveals your sins while binding you deeper into their embrace."

I shook my head wildly, a tempest of dread and defiance crashing within me. "You're a snake! You slither among the dead, whispering sweet lies while burying them in deceit!"

Arthur's gaze turned steely, a sudden chill settling between us as shadows tightened around him like protective vices. "It is you who are entangled in your own web, Jack. And it is your choices that have led to this inevitable confrontation." His voice lowered, reverberating with an unsettling finality. "Your soul cries out for release—let it flow through your quill."

Everything went black as a journal was thrust into my hands.

I woke back in the cell, confused and remembering exactly what Arthur said.

"Allow your pen to bleed the truth."

I will show them the truth, they are condemning an innocent man to death! I will show them that the true monsters of Whitechapel are still out there.

The journal lay heavy on my lap, its leather cover cold as the stones beneath me. My fingers trembled as they brushed against its spine, an electric pulse coursing through me, igniting a twisted fervor within my mind. I fumbled for the quill, its nib sharp and waiting to carve my revelations into the waiting emptiness.

I took a breath, the stench of despair wrapping around me like a shroud, and began to write. Words flowed like blood from a freshly opened wound, gushing forth in a torrent of agony and defiance:

> I am no monster. This infernal wretchedness seeps from the very streets that birthed it. The shadows dance with secrets, but they are not mine! Mine is but the truth—the cries of the innocent burdened by a darkness far more potent than what they've conjured in their fevered imaginations.

As I scribbled furiously, each word felt like a talisman against the encroaching madness that threatened to consume me whole. The rhythms of my own torment resonated within the pages. Each sentence a prayer to some unseen deity of mercy, each scratch of ink an invocation against the whispers that haunted my nights.

But soon, tendrils of doubt crept in, twisting around my resolve like vines choking the life from a flower. Morgana's laughter echoed faintly in the recesses of my mind; her voice slithered through my thoughts like smoke.

"Your words are sweet poison, Jack. How delicious it is to watch you writhe under the weight of your own illusions."

I shook my head violently, attempting to banish her haunting presence. "Leave me be!" I cried into the suffocating stillness of my cell, casting furtive glances at the shadows that lurked just beyond the flickering candlelight. Yet her spectral form lingered just out of sight, her whispering taunts growing louder as I sank deeper into this manic spiral.

"Ahhh," she crooned seductively, "the truth? Tell me —what truth is worth redeeming? The world knows only fear and deception. You are but marionette strings pulled by hands unseen."

"No!" My voice cracked as I fought back against her malevolence. "They will see... they will understand! Arthur can't control me!"

But doubt gnawed at the edges of my conviction. What if it was all in vain? What if they were right? My mind raced with visions of knives glinting under gaslight —shadows lurking at every corner—and I could almost feel their icy grip tightening around my throat.

I continued writing, each stroke both liberating and maddening as Arthur's words replayed in my mind. "We will weave a tapestry..." I paused, staring down at what I had scribed thus far—a jumble of manic claims and declarations—but suddenly clarity emerged from chaos.

"No," I whispered fiercely. "Not just claims... truths!" With renewed vigor, I poured everything onto those pages; tales of shadows skittering in alleyways, ghostly figures flitting past, whispers beckoning from candlelit corners where dread thrived, names buried under layers of grime and secrecy—the true predators hiding behind masks of civility.

And then came the moment of revelation—the chilling realization that I was not merely writing to exonerate myself. No, the ink bled something far more sinister. A reckoning of my own creation, a mirror reflecting the abyss I had embraced. The shadows knitted tighter around me, tendrils of darkness reaching forth to entwine my very essence.

With each stroke of the quill, I unearthed memories long buried beneath the weight of guilt. Flashes of laughter mingled with crimson stains upon cobblestones; familiar faces twisted in fear, their screams echoing through dampened streets in the dead of night. Morgana's whispers coiled around those recollections, demanding acknowledgment.

"You cannot escape yourself, Jack. You are as entwined with their fates as your own."

"No!" I cried out, desperation clawing at my throat like a noose drawn tight. "They were not my victims! The shadows meant to consume me are mere reflections of their own sins."

Yet, doubt darted in and out like a specter, a vengeful spirit demanding recompense. Each paragraph unveiled not merely tales of terror but slivers of my fractured psyche, my identity unraveling before my eyes, a kaleidoscope of anguish and despair.

And then came Arthur's voice again, soft yet laced with venom. "An innocent man? Or merely a monster hidden behind the mask of sanity?" His presence loomed larger than the cell itself. Each heartbeat echoed like a law unto itself in this oppressive silence. I could feel his gaze boring into my soul as if he were peeling away layers to expose the festering core beneath.

The journal pulsed with an energy of its own, demanding more than just confessions; it sought a reckoning that transcended this wretched prison cell. I scribbled madly once more, feverish abandon giving way to an unearthly purpose.

Listen closely! For you will know my torment, and perhaps understand that the true monsters walk among you still! They wear well-tailored suits and present themselves with disarming smiles while darkness festers just beneath their skin.

I glanced up abruptly, sweat beading on my brow as heavy footfalls echoed down the corridor outside. The door creaked open slowly, and a figure stepped through the threshold—a silhouette framed by flickering light. Arthur stood there, impeccably dressed and yet utterly wretched in his predatory calm.

"Ah," he said, voice smooth as silk but edged with steel, "how delightfully lost you seem in your own labyrinthine thoughts." He stepped closer, and the air thickened. Morgana's laughter rose like fog from unseen depths.

"Stop!" I shouted, brandishing my quill like a dagger against the mounting dread coiling in my gut. "You cannot claim me—the truth is mine to wield!"

Chapter Nine
The Writing Desk

November 13, 1888

The candle sputtered, casting long, flickering shadows across the cold stone walls of my cell. I watched the light wane, its fight to stay alive a reflection of my own fleeting days. I dipped the quill into the ink, the black liquid swirling like the memories I sought to exorcize. The tip scratched across the rough paper, and in the silence of my prison, I finished my story.

They think they know me.

I wrote, my hand steady despite the tremor in my chest.

*They've painted me a monster, a beast
lurking in the shadows, knife at the ready.
But there are shadows far darker than me,
and horrors that even I fear.*

My fingers tightened around the quill, smearing ink across the page. The room grew colder, as though the very act of writing the final pages summoned something from the darkness beyond.

I glanced over my shoulder, an old habit now, expecting to see the wraiths that had followed me for so long. The walls stood bare, but my skin prickled with the sensation of being watched. Always watched. I shuddered and forced my gaze back to the paper.

Outside the cell of my imagination, the streets of London were alive with fear. The fog clung to the cobblestones, swirling around the feet of those brave enough to walk into Whitechapel after dark.

The murders had ceased with my capture, but the city still whispered my name, cursed me for the blood that had soaked its streets.

But they were mistaken.

The first had appeared in the winter of '88. A woman, throat slashed, her body arranged with a precision that mirrored dark rituals I had read about in forbidden tomes. I had stood above her, not as the killer, but as a witness to something older, something that didn't belong in this world.

My quill paused, hovering over the paper. The

memory of that night was vivid—too vivid. I could still smell the blood, still feel the frigid breath of the creature that had slithered away before anyone else arrived. It had eyes, though. Eyes that glowed faintly in the dark, reflecting the gas lamps like a predator's gaze.

No one believes the truth.

I wrote, the scratch of my quill growing sharper, more frantic.

No one will understand that I fought them. That I tried to stop the horrors. They think I am the horror.

The laugh that escaped my lips was bitter, twisted. How could they understand? How could they know that the blade I carried wasn't for the women, but for the things that walked unseen, hunting through the mist?

It was after the third killing that I realized the truth. The police were closing in, the press rabid, screaming for blood. And in the shadows, the thing laughed. It was never seen, never heard by others, but I felt it. Every night. Following me, taunting me.

And on that night, I saw its face.

My breath hitched as I recalled the twisted, eyeless visage. It was human-shaped, but wrong—skin too pale, stretched over bone like wet paper. Its mouth had no lips, just a slash of black. When it smiled, rows of jagged teeth caught the moonlight.

I hadn't been the one who killed that woman. But she had been dead long before my knife touched her. That thing had taken her soul. I knew it, and yet... the knife had been in my hand. Blood on my clothes. My mind screamed that I wasn't responsible, but the voice in the back of my skull whispered otherwise.

The scratching of my quill slowed, and I stared at the page, my own words glaring back at me.

> *I was never the monster. I fought the monster. But hadn't the blood felt warm? Hadn't the knife felt so right in my hand, the blade sliding effortlessly through the skin?*

I slammed the quill down, ink splattering the paper. It wasn't me. It wasn't me.

The door to my cell creaked open. A guard stepped in, his eyes flicking over me with a mixture of disgust and fear. "They say you'll swing in the morning," the guard said, his voice thick with contempt. "They've got your gallows built and ready."

I didn't look up, my fingers clenched around the pen. "They think they're killing a murderer," I murmured, my voice hollow. "But they'll never know what's still out there, what walks those streets now that I'm locked away."

The guard snorted, shaking his head. "You're mad. Talking about demons and shadows. You've been chasing ghosts, Ripper. Maybe they'll follow you to hell."

My lips curled into a thin smile. The guard didn't know. None of them did. I'd seen what no one else had, felt the icy fingers of death that reached out from beyond. What was hell but a shadow of London, crawling with creatures too dark to see in daylight?

"Perhaps," I whispered, my eyes gleaming in the dim candlelight. "Perhaps they already have."

The door slammed shut behind the guard, leaving me alone with the silence again. I exhaled slowly and dipped my quill once more into the ink. My hand moved with newfound purpose, the words pouring from me like blood from an open wound.

They'll never believe me. They'll call me mad. But I fought the shadows for them. And I will die with their sins on my hands.

The candle flickered again, a gust of cold air slipping through the barred window. I paused, my gaze drifting toward the small square of night sky beyond. I imagined the fog rolling in again, impenetrable, swallowing the city whole. Inside that fog, the wraith would walk. It would find new prey. It always did.

I smiled grimly, letting the words come, my final confession etched in ink, the truth buried between lines of madness.

Let them think I was the Ripper. It's better they believe that than face what truly walks among them.

The quill stopped, the ink drying in the grooves of

the paper. I leaned back, my chest rising and falling slowly, a man who had found peace in the chaos of his mind. Tomorrow, they will hang me. They would think they had ended the nightmare.

But the nightmare wasn't mine to end.

And as the last flicker of the candle extinguished itself, I let the darkness embrace me, a faint whisper of a smile still on my lips.

Let them believe the story.

CHAPTER TEN
FINALE

London Evening Gazette
November 14, 1888
Jack the Ripper Hanged: The Madman Who Believed in Shadows Meets His End.
By: Henry P. Alcott

In what will undoubtedly be remembered as one of the most significant days in London's history, Jack the Ripper, the fiend who terrorized the streets of Whitechapel for months, was finally brought to justice. This morning, at precisely 8:00 AM, Johnathan "Jack" Ainsley was hanged at Newgate Prison for the brutal murders of five women—crimes that will forever remain etched in the annals of this city's darkest days.

The culmination of months of panic, fear, and wild speculation, Ainsley's capture came after a harrowing manhunt that gripped the entire city. A former doctor's assistant, Ainsley had long been hiding in plain sight, his face that of a respectable man, but his mind ravaged by delusions. Court documents revealed chilling details about his mental state—obsessed with shadows and specters he claimed to see stalking the streets of London. His belief that supernatural forces were behind the murders only added to his infamy, blurring the lines between madman and monster.

At his trial, Ainsley repeatedly maintained that he was not the killer, but merely an "observer," hunting down what he called "the shadows." His disjointed rants of demons and phantoms unnerved those present, casting him not only as a cold-blooded murderer but also as a man lost in the labyrinth of his own mind. His unreliability as a narrator of his own life made his defense impossible. The jury deliberated for a mere 15 minutes before delivering a unanimous verdict: guilty.

The mystery surrounding Ainsley began to unravel after the police found a bizarre manuscript in his cell, half-written and filled with incoherent ramblings about dark forces he believed had infiltrated the city. The manuscript described grisly murders eerily similar to those for which he was charged, but his writings blurred reality and fantasy. Ainsley's delusion that he was not the true perpetrator, but rather chasing a supernatural force, was nothing more than the twisted workings of a frac-tured mind.

Ainsley's unraveling began long before his capture, though the world did not know it at the time. Friends, few that they were, recall him as a man haunted by some-thing more than just the hardships of life. His descent into madness, they say, was rapid, though carefully concealed behind a mask of civility. Neighbors reported seeing him pacing his small flat at odd hours, mumbling to himself, and obsessively drawing strange symbols on the walls. He became convinced that the fog rolling off the Thames carried with it creatures from another world —phantoms that compelled him to kill.

But it was not phantoms that prowled the streets. It was Ainsley himself, knife in hand, seeking to satisfy whatever insatiable need had seized him. Though he insisted until his last breath that he acted under supernatural compulsion, the evidence painted a far more chilling picture. Ainsley, in a calculated frenzy, stalked his victims—women of the night, vulnerable and alone— luring them into dark alleys before striking with clinical precision. The savagery of the murders, coupled with the calculated dissection of their bodies, revealed a mind coldly focused on his heinous task.

In his final days, as he awaited the hangman's noose, Ainsley remained detached from reality, speaking only of shadows that whispered to him in the night. His few visitors—psychiatrists and priests—reported that Ainsley showed no remorse, not because he did not feel guilt, but because he genuinely believed that he was never in control of his actions.

Today, as Jack the Ripper is consigned to history, the streets of Whitechapel can begin to heal. The terror that has gripped this city for so long begins to lift, and with it, the lives of those taken by this monster are finally given their due respect. The women who fell prey to his madness—Mary Ann Nichols, Annie Chapman, Elizabeth Stride, Catherine Eddowes, and Mary Jane Kelly—shall not be remembered as mere victims, but as daughters, sisters, and mothers whose lives were stolen by a madman's violent delusions.

Whitechapel itself, stained by the blood of these innocent women, breathes a little easier today. The public mourns for the women who were cast aside in life, whose names have been eclipsed by the notoriety of their killer. But let it be known, it is they who deserve remembrance.

The memorial service for these women is set for next week, and a public gathering is expected at the corner of Hanbury Street where Annie Chapman was found, to pay respects and acknowledge the grief that has settled over London since the first body was discovered.

For too long, the shadow of Jack the Ripper loomed large over Whitechapel. But now, with his death, the city has a chance to reclaim itself, and to finally honor those who fell to his blade. May their souls rest in peace, and may this chapter of horror be forever closed.

As Ainsley's body hung limp on the gallows this morning, the crowd gathered outside Newgate was eerily silent. The tension of relief hung in the air—relief that this reign of terror had finally come to an end. But with that relief came a sense of sadness. The lives lost could never be returned, and the scars on this city, physical and emotional, would never truly fade.

For those who witnessed his hanging, there were no cheers, no cries of victory. Only a quiet, collective exhale. The man who believed in shadows was no more. And yet, those who peered into his eyes in the final moments swear they saw something there—something that chilled them to the bone.

Jack the Ripper, the madman of Whitechapel, is dead. But his legend, his darkness, will linger, like the fog that still rolls through the streets, whispering of things unseen. Let us never forget the women who were lost to this madness:

Mary Ann Nichols, Annie Chapman, Elizabeth Stride, Catherine Eddowes, Mary Jane Kelly and others who fell under the madman's grasp.

May their names outlive his.

Epilogue
The Fog

The fog had returned, thicker than ever, curling through the streets of Whitechapel like a living thing. It clung to the brick walls, suffocating the gas lamps, and swallowing the few souls who dared to venture out after dusk. There were whispers again—whispers of something lurking just beyond the mist, watching, waiting.

The city had begun to heal after Jack the Ripper's hanging, or so it seemed. But those who had witnessed the execution, those who had looked into the killer's eyes as the noose tightened around his neck, spoke of something unsettling. They said that as Ainsley's body dropped, his lips had moved. No sound escaped, but some claimed to have seen it—a smirk, a fleeting smile that vanished as quickly as it came.

What did it mean?

The newspapers had declared the case closed, the monster dead. Yet, in the darkest corners of Whitechapel, rumors still stirred. There were those who whispered that the murders had been something more than the work of a man, that Ainsley's madness was not his own. They spoke of shadows—things that slithered through the fog, unseen, but always there, always watching. Ainsley had spoken of them in his final days, hadn't he? Shadows that drove him to madness, to murder. But that was the rambling of a madman, wasn't it?

Or was it?

A figure moved through the fog now, his coat flapping like the wings of a bird. He walked the same streets Jack the Ripper had once prowled, his footsteps soft on the cobblestones. His breath came out in clouds of mist, but his eyes... his eyes seemed distant, as though he were looking through the fog, into something else. Something unseen.

He stopped at a familiar spot, the place where the first body had been found. Mary Ann Nichols. Her name had been carved into history, but here, in the silence of the night, it felt as though the city had forgotten her. The man bent down, touching the ground, his fingers grazing the cold stone as if searching for something.

A gust of wind swept through the alley, and with it came a sound—low, faint, but unmistakable. A whisper.

His heart pounded in his chest, a chill running down his spine. He turned sharply, eyes scanning the darkness. There was no one there. Of course, there was no one there. But the whisper came again, clearer this time, and closer.

Jack?

The man froze. The name hung in the air, disembodied, soft like a lover's sigh. He turned back to the ground where his fingers had brushed the cobblestones. For the briefest of moments, he thought he saw something—a shadow darker than the fog, slipping through the cracks in the stone, disappearing into the earth.

His breath quickened. It was impossible. The killer was dead. Everyone had seen it. *Jack the Ripper is dead.*

But then why did the fog feel so alive tonight? Why did it feel like it was watching him, pressing in closer, whispering secrets from the shadows?

He stood, shaking off the unease, but as he turned to leave, he felt a presence behind him. A cold, invisible hand grazing the back of his neck. He spun around, but again, nothing. Just the fog, curling like smoke in the night.

"You wear their guilt as your flesh..."

The voice echoed in his mind, faint but familiar. He knew that voice. The voices of the women, the victims. Hadn't they all spoken to him in his dreams? In the dark hours, when he lay awake, haunted by images of blood and torn flesh? He had never been able to forget them. Could it be...?

Ainsley had spoken of shadows—creatures from another world, things that whispered and commanded. But Ainsley was mad. He was delusional. Or was he? Could the Ripper have been telling the truth all along? Could it have been the shadows, twisting his mind, using him as a puppet?

The man took a step back, his head spinning. The fog

thickened, and within it, he thought he saw movement—a figure, faint but there. It hovered at the edge of the mist, watching him.

"Who's there?" his voice shook, though he tried to sound strong.

The figure didn't answer. It just stood there, barely visible through the haze. And then, slowly, it smiled. Not a kind smile, not a warm one. It was the same smile he had seen on Ainsley's face just before the hangman's noose had snapped his neck.

The next morning, the fog lifted, as it always did. The city awoke, the streets filling once more with the sound of carriages and footfalls. But for those who knew where to look, there was something different in the air.

Another body had been found in the alleyways of Whitechapel.

The police, of course, dismissed it as unrelated. A simple street killing, a robbery gone wrong, they said. The Ripper was dead. But those who remembered, those who had seen the shadows, whispered among themselves.

The fog was returning, and with it, the whispers.

Was it Jack, back from the dead? Or had it always been something else, something darker, lurking in the mist, using men like Ainsley as its hands?

No one could say for sure. But as the fog rolled in

again that night, thicker and darker than ever before, one thing was certain:

The shadows were not done with Whitechapel. And perhaps, just perhaps, they never had been.

Afterword

Dear Reader,

If you've made it this far, I hope you've felt the unsettling chill of the fog creeping through Whitechapel, the blurred lines between reality and madness, and the overwhelming weight of ambiguity that hangs over this story. I wanted to take a moment to address something important: this novel was never written to glorify Jack the Ripper, nor to romanticize the horrors he committed. Instead, it's a deliberate exploration of a deeply fractured mind—a descent into madness where truth and delusion are intertwined so tightly that even the reader cannot be certain where one ends and the other begins.

The ending is, by design, ambiguous. Did the shadows exist, manipulating the killer? Or were they merely a manifestation of a deranged mind, a convenient scapegoat for atrocities too monstrous to face? I leave that for you to decide. The goal was to step into the shoes of a man lost in his own darkness, consumed by paranoia and the terror of forces—real or imagined—that he could not escape.

But above all, this story is a tribute to the women whose lives were brutally stolen. The real women who lived, breathed, and loved in London's East End, only to have their stories overshadowed by a nameless monster. Mary Ann Nichols, Annie Chapman, Elizabeth Stride, Catherine Eddowes, and Mary Jane Kelly—these were human beings, each with a life and a voice, and they deserve to be remembered as such.

This novel does not seek to mythologize the Ripper, but to show the raw horror of his actions and to reflect on the humanity of those who suffered because of them. If the ambiguity leaves you unsettled, I hope it also reminds you that history itself is often unclear, leaving us to grapple with more questions than answers.

Thank you for reading, and may we never forget the names of the victims, long after the moniker of the killer is erased from history.

— Ryen

Acknowledgments

I'll keep this one short, as there are so many people I want to thank that it would be longer than this book itself LOL. I'm foregoing any semblance of grammar, sentence structure and more here, so hang on.

To Oaky, our sweet $25 pandemic puppy from the animal shelter in Knoxville, TN. Cancer is a bitch. I love you and miss you so much buddy. You gave us a great 4 years and I wouldn't take back any second even though the heartbreak is immeasurable. This book is born from insomnia induced heartbreak over the loss of you and I'm sorry it turned out this grim. I miss you my oaky-dokey. You gave chemo a helluva shot and I'm grateful we could provide that for you. The extra year and a half was worth every cent.

To Hendrix, thank you for staying asleep while Mom wrote this so I could disassociate and get into this messed up headspace. I love you buddy, I love you always, I love you forever.

To Anthony, thank you for helping me through all of this. There is no one else I'd rather take on the journey of life with. Through grief, stress, joy, and everything in between. I love you.

To my aunt Michele, kick the fuck out of cancers ass.

To my editor Stacey, and Ashleigh, thank you both for reading outside your genre and testing out this little mind-fuck. Even though spooky stories give you both heart palpitations hahaha.

To Jess, Hallie, Tobiah, Addison, Ashleigh, and everyone else in Smutty Meme Hoes, thank you for your support. I love you all so dearly.

To my family both blood and found, thank you all for your support.

To everyone taken before their time, and by the hands of others. May you rest in peace and know you're never forgotten.

And finally, to you. My readers. I wouldn't be here without you.

Grateful for all of you,
Ryen.

About the Author

Ryen Santana is an accidental night owl who seizes moments for writing during her son's nap times and bedtime, fueled by coffee and unwavering determination.

Her journey began with writing Twilight fan fictions on Wattpad (though, unfortunately, they're long gone now). From those early, cringy fan fictions emerged a desire to craft something more substantial. During the throes of early motherhood, Ryen decided to turn her passion for storytelling into something more serious.

"Sanguine" is Ryen's debut psychological thriller.

When not lost in writing or sharing books with her husband and son, she enjoys quiet moments with her dogs and long walks in Copenhagen, Denmark where she currently resides.

www.ryenwrites.io

instagram.com/ryenwrites

tiktok.com/@ryenlsantana